MW00946295

This book is dedicated to Heather and the Wee Ones. Also, to all the family and friends who have followed and supported *The Massive Stone* over the last thirty years.

www.mascotbooks.com

The Massive Stone

©2016 Scott Walker. All Rights Reserved. No part of this publication may be reproduced, stored in a retrieval system or transmitted in any form by any means electronic, mechanical, or photocopying, recording or otherwise without the permission of the author.

For more information, please contact:
Mascot Books
560 Herndon Parkway #120
Herndon, VA 20170
info@mascotbooks.com

Library of Congress Control Number: 2016908666

CPSIA Code: PRT0716A
ISBN-13: 978-1-63177-580-2

Printed in the United States

THE MASSIVE STONE

by **Scott Walker**   Illustrated by **Katie Mazeika**

The Massive Stone
    Sat all alone

In the park at the dawn of day,

And he thought,
    Though stones think not,

I wish I could move and play.

He sat there all morning,
All sad and forlorning,

And wasted the hours away.

Noon finally came,
     But Stone felt the same,

With gnawing self-pity inside.

Then a boy came along,
     Whistling a song,

And hopped on Stone for a ride.

When people came by,
    The boy was sly

And slid behind Stone to hide.

So Stone found a friend,
    With hours to spend,

And his joy started growing inside.

They played every fun game that they knew,

Then made some up and played them, too.

The boy was a pirate,
Stone his ship.

The boy was an astronaut
on a rocky space trip.

The boy was a cowboy with a horse of Stone,

And Stone was just happy he wasn't alone.

Soon the darkness was growing,
With an evening wind blowing,

And the boy had to go home for the night.

But, he said, "Stone's my friend,
And I'll be back again,

I promise, by first morning light."

And Stone smiled and thought,
Though stones smile not,

My, the moon's shining bright.

And that is the story of the Massive Stone,
Who found happiness and joy from a friend.

Whether massive or small,
We need friends, one and all.

That's the moral,
and it's also the end.